The Green Lady

a novella by

M. R. Williamson

The Green Lady
by M. R. Williamson

All rights reserved. No part of this book may be reproduced or transmitted in any form or by any means, electronic or mechanical, including photocopying or recording or by any information storage and retrieval systems, without expressed written consent of the author and/or artists.

The Green Lady is a work of fiction. Names, characters, places, and incidents are products of the author's imagination. Any resemblance to actual events or persons, living or dead, is entirely coincidental.

Story copyright owned by Marvin Williamson
Cover illustration "Green Ghost" by Marcia Borell
Cover design by Laura Givens

First Printing, May 2019
Second Printing, February 2024

Hiraeth Publishing
P.O. Box 1248
Tularosa, NM 88352
e-mail: hiraethsubs@yahoo.com
www.hiraethsffh.com

Visit www.hiraethsffh.com for online science fiction, fantasy, horror, scifaiku, and more. Stop by our online bookstore for novels, magazines, anthologies, and collections. **Support the small, independent press...and your First Amendment rights.**

Also by M. R. Williamson

Horned Jack: The Early Years*
Horned Jack: The Nephilim*
Horned Jack: Never Say Never*
Horned Jack: Pound of Flesh
The Pragamore Chronicles
Bridges into the Imagination*
Bridges into the Imagination 2*
Bridges into the Imagination 3*
Curse of the Monkey's Paw*
Can You See Me?*
I, Gnome*he Angel of Holloway
The Stone Collector
The Moleskin Cap
Mysterious Rider*

* published by Hiraeth Publishing

The Green Lady

Part 1
One of a Hundred

Birmingham Jones, the Elmore's handyman, stood in the back yard at the cattle gap, staring at the old barn. Although a faded red it was from far too many seasons, the cypress still remained strong and resilient. The old, colored man and his wife, Mrs. Emily, had been with the Elmore family even before Brice and Heather were married. But now, with the inheritance of the old, Easley farm place, their chores have expanded somewhat. With the passing of the Great Depression, the old farm provided a much more economical place for the

Elmores. . . .

"My-my," complained Birmingham as he stared at the shoulder-high hogweed, golden rods and Johnson grass in the front, barn lot. "I'd be most satisfied bein' the 'round the house maintenance man," he grumbled. I could sure do without these 'round the barn, chicken coop, chop the wood, and fix the wagon things."

"Birmingham!"

The call was not only loud, it had a touch of impatience laced in with it.

"Yes, Ma'am." Birmingham turned to see Mrs. Emily standing at the back porch, holding the screen door open.

"Don't jus' stand there, Mr. B. That loft door ain't gonna fix itself. Young Hunter get caught up in that thing it'll be the Devil to pay."

"Yes Ma'am. I know they gonna be back from Tupelo tomorrow, two days before Halloween. I got the pumpkins on the porch jus' like you said. They got faces and candles and everything. When I get this trap door fixed, I'll make the corn stalk tents for some of 'em in the yard."

"Good," agreed Mrs. Emily. "Some o' those decorations are in the barn loft. Mr. Brice said Mrs. Easily kept 'em in a big, ole, wooden footlocker."

"Got it," said Birmingham as he sidled through the cattle gap.

Continuing toward the barn, he dodged the occasional yellow ragweed that the breeze occasionally leaned too close. Slowing, he checked the back porch. Mrs. Emily was still there and waving him on.

"My, my," he complained as he continued toward the barn. "I'll bet that old box is older than I am."

In little time, the old handyman had removed the hinges and hand drilled the new pilot holes for the new screws. Being still solid, the old door worked out well for him. Slowly turning, he now eyed the old, wooden trunk-of-a-thing sitting toward the house in the far, right corner. It was directly across from where Mrs. Easley had the field hand pile the hay. Unfortunately, it was the same place where young Hunter had caught the huge chicken snake. He eyed the huge stacks of hay.

"All right all you creepy-crawlies, four-legged and no-legged vermin, I got 'a cotton choppin' hoe downstairs. I'll put more dents in your hide than you can get over in a year."

Gingerly moving over the loose hay on the floor, he eased toward the far end of the loft, eying the darker corners carefully.

"I know you here Elmer," said Birmingham at a whisper. "Nobody names a snake Elmer 'cept Hunter."

He stopped within but a reach of the old locker. It had a dusty, folded, burlap bag, on its top. Carefully taking it, he shook the dust from the bag, folded it in half, and then twisted it into something that resembled a club. Easing his left hand to the chest latch, he tripped it and then slowly opened the lid.

"Well. . ." he managed with a touch of relief. "We got plastic pumpkins, bags of rubber bats and spiders, rolls of fake cobwebs, and black and orange candles."

Quickly putting the decorations in his bag, he started to close the lid when something caught his eye--a light reflecting off of something wedged in the far right corner of the box. It glittered with a bright, gold color. Quickly pulling out his pocket knife, he opted for a short, stout blade, and then carefully pried the gold coin from the crack.

"Well, I'll just be dumbfounded," he said, rolling the half-dollar sized coin between his thumb and forefinger, "A 1849 Double Eagle."

"Birmingham?"

The call from the bottom of the ladder came more in the form of a question, causing the old handyman to stop and look toward the loft door.

"Yes Ma'am," replied Birmingham.

"Please tell me you've found that old trunk," said Mrs. Emily.

"Yep. Got 'em all packed up and with a surprise to boot," he answered.

Birmingham eased the top down on the old trunk, shouldered the burlap bag, and then walked briskly back to the still open floor door.

"Jus' let 'em down easy to me, Mr. B and don't drop 'em," she instructed as she reached up for the bag.

Following Mrs. Emily's advice, Birmingham knelt on his right knee and eased the bag through the opening and into her waiting hands. His grin looked totally out of place.

Mrs. Emily sat the bag down and moved aside as Birmingham stepped down the ladder. "What are you grinnin' for? It's almost 9:30AM an' we got a ton of work to be done afore dark. Sunday, this place gonna look like All Saint's Eve an' I need your help in the kitchen. We got a fresh-cut beef roast an' I need you ta trim it and get the vegetables ready for the pot."

"No problem," replied Birmingham. "Jus' a few finishin' touches with this stuff an' Weepin' Willows gonna be ready for the Elmores. I think." He reached into his right pocket and pulled out the coin. "What do you make of this?" he asked, holding it out to her in his palm.

Mrs. Emily squinted at the coin, almost afraid to touch it. "Is it real?" She gingerly took it from his hand. "It's got 1849 on it but it looks brand new." Her squint held as she looked back up at him. "Where'd you find it?"

Birmingham shrugged with, "It was wedged into a crack between the bottom and the side of the old trunk."

"How much is it worth do you think?"

"Not sure," replied Birmingham. "It's a Double Eagle. Haven't seen many of those in my lifetime. I remember way back in the thirties, President Roosevelt tried to get 'em all and melt 'em down."

"Well. . ." Mrs. Emily shook her head as she judged the gold coin's weight. "He certainly didn't get this one. Think it's worth a hundred?"

Birmingham shrugged again. "The Good Lord only knows, Mrs. Emily. Five or six probably." He slowly looked up at his wife. "You know this really ain't ours."

"'Corse I do, Mr. B. But it sure might help Mr. Brice with things 'round here."

☊ ☊ ☊

That evening, a Saturday and about 7:30PM, the rigors of the day had put Birmingham deep in his old recliner and halfway through the second of Mrs. Emily's cheeseburgers. While staring at the television, the Ed Sullivan show had slowly lost its grip on the old fellow. Birmingham's head began to nod as his eyelids grew increasingly heavy. . . .

"Mr. B?"

The hale from the kitchen was like the bell ringing on round ten, but the boxer was still lying on the canvas.

Birmingham dropped the unfinished burger on the plate in his lap and screwed the top back on the bottle of Ripple Wine. "Yes Ma'am. What can I do for you right now?" he added politely.

"Jus' take out the garbage before the bottom of the sack gets so wet it won't hold it please," explained Mrs. Emily. "It's gettin' dark early, cloudin' up. I believe a storm's comin'. I can see it flash up in the west now and then, but I don't hear the thunder."

"Uh huh," replied Birmingham weakly.

Getting up with his plate, he walked slowly to the kitchen and traded it with Mrs. Emily for the sack of garbage. With plate in hind, she opened the door to the porch that connected the servant's quarters with the main house. Birmingham stepped outside, letting the screen door ease shut.

"Dreariest Saturday evening I've seen in a while," he managed, looking out across the almost dark, back yard. "The air's heavy. I smell rain and there ain't a leaf movin' on the old ash in the back yard."

Birmingham stood there, watching the lightening play among the thunderheads in the west. As he did, one of the double doors in the front of the old barn slowly opened. Not seeing a soul, he stood there staring at the darkness inside the barn. Then, as if in a dream, the back door of the main house swung open and out stepped a blond-haired lady in a long, pale green dress. She stood there for a moment with her matching bonnet hiding her face. But before the old maintenance man could decide just what to do, the air was filled with laughter. Maniacal it sounded, like that of someone possessed. Birmingham dropped the paper sack to the porch. Hearing the sack hit the wooden porch, the lady quickly turned toward the servant's quarters. Birmingham's eyes grew big, for there were no features to see--no eyes, no mouth, and not a sign of a nose.

Laughing again, it leaped from the porch and ran toward the barn with the speed of a deer to disappear into the darkness inside.

"Birmingham!"

The old fellow jumped at the loud scolding from inside.

Mrs. Emily paused inside by the screen door. "Did you drop that. . ."

"Yes. . .and then, no," answered Birmingham, still staring at the now closed barn door.

Mrs. Emily quickly stepped out onto the porch with a broom in one hand and another paper bag in the other. "What's this yes and no stuff? You're the onliest somebody out here."

"I wish I was." Birmingham's voice weak.

Mrs. Emily eased up beside her husband, looking toward the barn also. "Why were you laughing?"

Birmingham slowly shook his head. "Wasn't me. I never made a sound, 'cept my heart beatin' like a drum."

"Then who did?" asked Mrs. Emily, noting that her husband's gaze was still on the barn.

"The whoever that was in the house. She ran out, across the back yard, through the cattle gap, and right into the barn."

"A woman?" Mrs. Emily slowly turned, squinting at her husband.

Birmingham slowly nodded. "She glowed green all over and didn't have a face at all."

"Glowed? No face?" echoed Mrs. Emily.

He nodded again, looking back at her. "She looked straight at me--no nose, no mouth, no eyes, no nothin'. Sounded like a. . . ."

"Banshee," guessed Mrs. Emily.

The weak nod came again.

"Wait right here." With that, Mrs. Emily wheeled and went back inside. In just seconds, she came back outside with a twelve inch, iron skillet in her right hand. "The back door's open, Mr. B. We can't jus' shut it. We got'ta check the house before we lock it back."

"My-my," groaned Birmingham weakly. "People jus' keep pushin' me where I had not rather go."

"Chin up, Mr. B," encouraged Mrs. Emily as she gently nudged him toward the still open, main house, back door. "A brave man is one who's scared but does the right thing anyways."

"Uh huh." Birmingham's comment week. "I ain't John Wayne."

Pausing at the screen door, he slowly opened it, reached inside, and then pulled out a baseball bat. Smiling, he glanced back at his wife. "Louisville Slugger--Mrs. Anna's backbone." He glanced back at the barn. "What about--"

"Ain't goin' there right now." Her tone firm. "We need to check this house right now. Mr. Brice can check the barn tomorrow when they get back." She nudged his back again.

"We goin'. We goin'," grumbled Birmingham as he turned on the lights and eased into the kitchen.

"Check the dining room," said Mrs. Emily as she turned and locked the back door.

"Uh huh. . ." Birmingham eased on into the dining room and turned on the lights. Looking to his left, he eyed the stairway leading to the library and the girl's bedroom.

"Straight ahead, Mr. B," whispered Mrs. Emily. "Let's check the living room and the two bedrooms."

Birmingham eased on through the dining room, constantly eying the head of the stairway. Now, with Mrs. Emily standing fast near the dining room table, he turned on the light and eased on into the living room with the 'Slugger' cocked and ready. At that very instant, the old grandfather clock struck 8:00PM. The coil chimes broke the silence like a china plate dropped on a stone floor.

"Gracious me!" Birmingham wheeled, pointing the shaky bat at the old, cherry wood timepiece.

Eight, solid times it struck and then continued with a louder than usual tick-tock which seemed to echo throughout the old house.

Mr. B looked back at Mrs. Emily. "That sound normal to you?" he whispered.

"A weak 'Kind of,'" was all she could manage.

Birmingham slowly turned back to the old clock. But there was something a bit unusual about Mr. Christopher's pride and joy. It looked different somehow.

"Birmingham?" Mrs. Emily's voice weak.

Birmingham eased closer to the old clock. He heard her of course, but her voice sounded weak and far off. The closer he got, the more obvious became the difference. The face of the old time piece was no longer there—no hands, no brass pins to mark the days, and no numbers for the hours.

Mrs. Emily moved from the table to just inside the entrance way to the living room. "Birmingham?" she said just above a whisper.

But her husband's gaze was locked on the face of the clock, now just a short reach away.

"Birmingham!" she shouted. "You're scaring me!"

Birmingham instantly straightened up, briskly rubbed his face, and then looked back at the face of the clock. "He's gone, Mrs. Emily," came his very weak reply.

"He? Please, Mr. B. Let's jus' go back to our place. Maybe checking here was a bad idea after all."

"Directly," responded Birmingham as he backed away, glancing at the two bedrooms left of the front door.

"Watch them stairs and I'll check the bedrooms."

Mrs. Emily reluctantly nodded, tightening her grip of the frying pan.

In just minutes, Birmingham was back. But as they walked toward the bathroom to the right of the stairs, something fell to the floor above them.

Mrs. Emily jumped, looking to the top of the stairway. "What on earth was that?" she managed.

"Not a clue," whispered Birmingham, "but it sounded heavy."

"Right behind you," she whispered, tugging at his shirt for him to lead the way.

"Uh huh," replied Mr. B as he eased toward the base of the stairs.

Gaining that, he nodded to the bathroom. "Check that.

I'll watch these stairs."

Mrs. Emily gripped the fry pan with both hands, tiptoed to the bathroom, and then quickly returned. "Nobody," she whispered. "That sound from upstairs was almost right above us. That's Anna and Hailey's room." She slowly looked to Birmingham. "You know, that was Susan's old room also."

"There you go," grumbled Mr. B. "Jus' gotta bring ghosts into all this, don't ya?"

Mrs. Emily giggled as she stepped around her husband and eased up to the first step. Glancing back at him, she replied, "Didn't old Grandfather Christopher change your mind 'bout such things?"

"No," admitted Birmingham, "but he's still workin' on it."

Mrs. Emily eased up the stairway with Mr. B right behind her. Looking over her left shoulder, she had a good view through the banisters of the doorway to the girl's room as well as the storage area. Both were closed.

Mrs. Emily paused at the top of the stairs, eying the partially open door to the library at the right of the head of the stairs.

She glanced back at Mr. B. "What's this 'still' stuff? We all know he took little Susan back to Heaven with him and came right back for his wife that very, same day also. You were there."

"Yep. 'Fraid I was." He smiled at his wife. "You keep the dust off everything in the house. Right?"

"Sure I do. You know that." Mrs. Emily glanced back toward the girl's bedroom.

"Do you dust that big old clock or even set it?" asked Birmingham.

"Seldom needs it. Mrs. Heather probably does."

"Nope." Birmingham looked to the Library to his right. "I already asked her and Mr. Price too, and you know the girls never dust nothin'. That clock has seven, brass pins behind the pendulum inside the door marking each day of the week. It's wound every three days and the key is moved to the next day to be wound. But nobody in this family minds it. Seem strange to you?"

Mrs. Emily slowly shook her head. "Can't think on that now, Mr. B. Let's check the library, the girl's room, the storage room past it, and then get out of here."

"Watch the girl's room," whispered Birmingham. "Somethin' hit the floor just minutes ago and I don't think a ghost is that heavy."

Birmingham eased to the partially open library door and peeped inside. Slowly opening it wider, he quickly looked around and rejoined Mrs. Emily still at the head of the stairway.

15

"To the girl's room," he whispered as he took the lead again.

Following the banisters to the left and right above the stairway, Birmingham stopped just a reach from the door.

"Mr. B?" whispered Mrs. Emily as she held tight to the back of his shirt.

"Shhh. . ." he hissed. "Hear somethin' in there. Sounded like somethin' closed."

Slowly opening the door, Birmingham peeped inside. "Whew," he said softly. "Don't see a thing," he added, taking a deep breath.

Mrs. Emily pointed past him toward the closet. "Check that."

"Uh huh. . ." Birmingham glanced back at her. "Sure wish we had Hershey right now."

"Awww, go on Mr. B. He's with the Elmores right now."

"I know that. I know that." He looked at the closet door. "It's not closed," noted Mrs. Emily. "The girls never leave it like that."

"Know that too," replied Birmingham. He crept up to the door and slowly opened it.

"Would you just look at that," said Mrs. Emily, easing closer. "Nobody rummages through a summer clothes trunk in October.

"Rummage?" Birmingham slowly shook his head. "They scattered 'em all over the closet floor."

"Somebody's been here, Mr. B."

"Really," poked Birmingham. "Guess I missed that."

The poke earned him a painful pinch to his right side.

"Quit that," he responded, being as quiet as the moment would allow.

"C'mon, Mr. B," prompted Mrs. Emily. "Let's check the storage room and jus' leave this to Mr. Price."

"You got it," agreed Birmingham as he ushered his wife out of the bedroom.

Not wasting a second, the old maintenance man promptly marched to the next room, jerked the door open, and then took a quick half-step back.

"Nothin'."

But before he could turn to join Mrs. Emily, there came another loud bang-of-a-sound, seemingly from outside.

Birmingham jumped and then spun around, looking at the head of the stairs. "Bless my bald head. I know that sound. Come on!" he added loudly as he headed back along the banisters and toward the head of the stairs.

"Where we goin' now?" asked Mrs. Emily, not really trying to be quiet.

"Ain't but one somethin' makes a sound like that," explained Birmingham as he hurried down the stairway. "That's the two, big doors of the cellar. Somebody's down there right now."

"Birmingham?" Mrs. Emily continued to reach for his shirt, but kept missing it by only inches. Finally getting hold of it, she stopped him at the base of the stairway. "I ain't goin' in that dark place right nor or any other time. There's spiders as big as half a cantaloupe living in there."

Pulling away, Birmingham continued toward the back door in the kitchen. "Let's just take a look at the cellar doors."

In little time at all, the two were outside and walking toward the entrance to the cellar. Keeping a sharp eye on the barn, Birmingham paused at the heavy, slanted doors.

"There closed, Birmingham," noted Mrs. Emily. "Let's just go right now."

"Nope," whispered Birmingham. "I got'ta look. You keep an eye on that barn. If the door as much as juggles, let me know."

Holding the 'Slugger' in his right hand, Birmingham slowly opened the left door to the cellar and laid it back against the house.

"My-my," he said weakly, looking down into the darkness. "It's darker than the bottom of our well. If she was here, I don't see her right now."

"Can you see ghosts all the time?" asked Mrs. Emily as she watched him open the right door.

"Don't start," warned Birmingham. "I'm doin' better than average to get this far."

"Here." Mrs. Emily tapped his right arm with something.

Birmingham squinted. "A pin light?"

"C'mon Mr. B," she whispered. "Jus' take a quick look."

She snapped the light on, shining its narrow beam down into the cellar.

"Uh huh." Birmingham glanced at the barn and then took the light. "Keep watchin' that barn," he added as he slowly eased down the stairway. "A firefly got more light than this thing," he grumbled as he paused at the last of six steps.

Immediately to his left was the front wall. Stacked upon its shelves were more old dishes, cups, bowls, and saucers that one could imagine. It ran about ten feet to the left wall. It looked to contain all kinds of canned food in jars that looked as old as he was. Some were even sealed in lead, and with a content that time had drastically darkened. Looking on, he noticed at the back and right wall had no shelves. But stacked in front of them were bushel and peck baskets, old, cardboard, sealed boxes, and three, wooden kegs. Then, as if mustering up the last bit of courage he had left, he stepped out onto the floor.

But before taking another step, he began swinging his hands at something in front of him. "Look out!" he exclaimed.

Rubbing his head and face, pulling and slapping at his shirt and hair, Birmingham quickly backed up the steps and out of the root cellar.

"What in the world, Birmingham," said Mrs. Emily as she tried to keep her feet from under his brogans.

"Spider," he explained as he pulled the remaining cobwebs from his hair and shirt. "The one in my face was as big as a frog."

"Did it bite you?"

Birmingham slowly shook his head. "Didn't give 'em time."

"Well. . ." Mrs. Emily glanced at the barn. "The doors are still closed. Let's lock the back door to the main house and go back to our place. Mr. Brice can do what he wants tomorrow."

♎ ♎ ♎

Later that evening, Birmingham sat in his old recliner watching the ten o'clock news. The heavy eyelids were back again. . . .

"Mr. B," called Mrs. Emily from the bathroom. "If you stay up past eleven, I won't be able to pry you out o' bed in the mornin' and I'll need your help. Tupelo, Mississippi, ain't that far from Old Plank. Mr. Brice will have 'em all back here before noon I believe."

"Uh huh. . ." Birmingham slowly rubbed the feeling back in his face. "After all that jus' happened, it'll be a God-gifted wonder if I get any sleep at all tonight."

Mrs. Emily walked into the room in her navy blue robe and pink, fuzzy slippers. Stopping directly in front of his chair, she squinted. "You're not only talkin' 'bout that green lady are you? Why were you looking so hard at Mr. Christopher's old clock?"

Birmingham rested his head on the back of the chair and closed his eyes. "Cause it was lookin' back at me. That's why."

"Lookin at you?"

Birmingham nodded. "Remember when it struck eight?"

A slight nod came from Mrs. Emily.

"Well, it said something to me as it struck, or rather, Mr. Christopher did I think. 'You got one of a hundred, Birmingham Brown' he said. I moved as close to the old clock as my nerve would allow. Its face was gone like I said. Behind the glass looked to be a white cloud movin' all about. Then, from out o' that cloud floated a pair of gold, wire-rimmed glasses—his glasses. Slowly, little by little, his big, blue eyes appeared along with his face. 'At the rose of time', he said." Birmingham slowly shook his head as he looked at Mrs. Emily. "I jus' new he was back. Jus' knew he was still here, Mrs. Emily."

"Birmingham." Mrs. Emily placed a gentle hand on his shoulder. "He was tryin' to tell you somethin. What does all that mean?"

"Haven't a clew," grumbled Birmingham. "Jus' another puzzlement for Mr. Brice I suppose. He's the one who helps troubled folks with ghosts and stuff. He can puzzle over this Green Lady too."

"Sooo. . ." Mrs. Emily squinted. "You comin' to bed or not?"

Birmingham slowly nodded. "I'll try, but It ain't gonna be easy with what's past today."

Part 2
Unwanted Guest

The next morning, a cool and clear Friday on October 29th, a dull thud came from the kitchen to jar Birmingham from deep within his goose down pillow. Sitting up, he looked all about the bedroom and then out the open door toward into the hallway.

"Birmingham, you up?" came the query from the kitchen.

"Yep. . . You bet. Almost," he replied.

Wiping the sleep from his eyes, he slowly sat up on the side of the bed and looked at the Big Ben alarm clock.

"Ten after seven," he said weakly. "My-my. In all of my seventh two years, it took me this long to find out that ghosts are real. And now, when all is supposed to calm down a little, up jumps the Devil--a green one."

Ω Ω Ω

But it was a beautiful day in October for Birmingham. The Elmores arrived at 1:00Pm and true to form, with his help, Mrs. Emily had the huge, beef roast ready with potatoes, carrots and gravy. Birmingham's tale of the Green Lady, fit right in with the Halloween mood, especially for their nine-year-old son, Hunter and the girls. Hunter was glad to help inspect the barn with his father and Birmingham. Although their search turned up nothing, the biggest clue for Brice came from the most unexpected place—the garbage can at the rear of the servant's quarters. What Birmingham saw might have been contributed to the two, empty bottles of Ripple wine found there. But, true to form, Mrs. Emily came to the rescue with the strange goings-on about when they searched the main house after Birmingham's sighting. Thinking on that, Brice made a close inspection of the house and grounds but found not a clue. Then, that Friday evening, Anna was on her bed and reading a book when she noticed that Hershey, was sitting up close to

Hailey at the head of her bed. He was looking straight at their open closet. His low, almost muffled, growl quickly got her attention. . . .

"Anna," whispered Hailey.

Anna looked to her sister. She was staring at something in the closet also.

"Susan?" whispered Anna to her sister.

Hailey slowly shook her head. "Susan's no longer with us. Her grandfather took her back with him. Remember?"

"I know."

"Then come and look at this," whispered Hailey.

Anna eased out of the left side of her bed and on to the foot of her sister's with Hershey right behind her. The growl was still there. Then, as she neared the open closet, her eyes focused upon something written on the back wall. There, in two foot letters, 'GET OUT' was written in red paint. It was so fresh, the wet paint was still streaking down toward the floor. Hailey eased up beside Anna and pulled the light chain. The sixty watt bulb didn't make it any better. The writing looked like it had just been done.

Slowly backing from the closet, the two sisters screamed as they left the bedroom at a dead run with Hershey right behind them, barking like crazy.

"Slow down!" exclaimed Brice, now at the head of the stairway. "You'll trip and hurt yourselves."

"Someone's been in our bedroom," exclaimed Anna as the two stopped at the foot of the stairs.

"Come and see," added a much excited Hailey. "Whoever it was wrote 'Get Out' on the back wall of our closet in red paint."

"Paint?" Brice, now joined by Heather, quickly followed the girls upstairs to their bedroom with Mrs. Emily and Birmingham right behind them.

Knowing the room's previous reputation, Birmingham and Mrs. Emily paused at the doorway to watch.

Wasting not a second, Brice went straight to the still open closet. Stopping at the doorway, he squinted at the unwelcomed artwork. He glanced at the Labrador. "This place still has his attention."

"Brice?' Heather stepped closer, but stopped at the foot of Hailey's bed.

"Some kind of sick joke," grumbled Brice. He stepped into the closet and lightly touched the paint. Stepping back out of the closet, he held up his stained fingers to the others.

"Can't believe I missed it," said Mrs. Emily as she stepped forward, holding out a rag.

"You didn't," replied Brice, wiping his fingers. "It's still wet. Whoever did this was just here." He looked at the girls.

"We didn't see a thing," said Hailey with Anna shaking her head in agreement.

Birmingham eased past the others and peeped into the closet. "My-my," he complained. "Who would do a thing like this?"

"That might be a 'What'," said Anna. Her voice low.

"Get a pail of soapy water," suggested Heather, looking a Birmingham. "That might come off easier while it's still wet."

♎ ♎ ♎

Determined that there had been an intruder about, Brice searched the main house again. Being a solid six foot and two inches, and with a vast knowledge of the paranormal, he remained unjaded by Birmingham's tale of the Green Lady of Weeping Willows. Contact with the person, or entity is what he desired now and the quicker the better. He was just about to move his search to the barn when he paused at the base of the stairs.

"Birmingham!" he called loudly. "When you checked this place yesterday, did you include the attic?"

Birmingham walked briskly into the dining area. "No Sir, Mr. Brice. Guess it slipped our minds. Don't guess anyone has."

"Well. . ." Brice started up the stairs. "We'll just do that right now."

"My-my. . ."

The old handyman followed Brice up the stairway and halfway down the bannisters toward the girl's room, eying the pull-down staircase.

"Think something's there?" asked Hailey as she and Anna watched from their bedroom doorway.

Brice glanced at his daughters. "Don't know yet," he answered as the pulled down the stairs. "Where's Hershey?"

"In here," answered Anna. "He's still watching the closet and nobody's there."

"My, my," grumbled Birmingham again. "No body. Ain't that just it?"

"Don't you start," said Brice, laughing silently.

Mrs. Emily eased from the bedroom with a pail in her hand. "It came off fairly easy, Mr. Brice, and the old paint is still holdin."

Brice looked back up and toward the attic.

"Would you like me to take a look, Mr. Brice," asked Birmingham with that 'Please turn me down.' expression.

"Thanks, Mr. B, but I got this." He looked at the girls. "Where's Hunter?"

Hailey smiled. "Mom's got him cleaning the back porch."

"Cleaning?" echoed Brice through a squint.

Anna nodded. "It seems he sealed the cracks between the boards with mud, made a ring for his marble game, and then filled it with Mom's garden soil."

"I see," replied Brice as he eased up the stairs, stopping half way. "Please get me a flashlight, Mr. B," he asked.

"Gim'me a minute."

Birmingham turned and hurried down the stairway. In short time, he was back up with a three-cell Everyready.

"Mr. Brice. . ." Birmingham held to the shaky staircase, holding the flashlight up to him.

Brice took the light and then smiled down at him. "Just stay right there for me, Birmingham. You've seen this thing. Now I want a look at it."

"Fine. . ." Birmingham's voice weak. "But if she comes down this here ladder, It's gonna be powerful hard for me to stay put."

The girls laughed, but remained satisfied to watch from their doorway.

Now, with flashlight in hand, Brice eased up the ladder until his shoulders were even with the attic floor. Directing the beam to the wall in front of him, he slowly moved it clockwise around the attic. Most of it was floored and had everything from a baby bed and Christmas decorations, to neatly stacked boxes and old, folding chairs. Now pausing the beam at the space directly above the girl's bedroom, he found nothing unusual about it. He stepped on to the attic floor and was about to look closer when someone yelled 'Get out!'. The voice was shrill and high-pitched and he didn't recognize it at all. The girls screamed just as a door slammed shut downstairs with a resounding boom.

"Birmingham!" Brice instantly looked down the ladder to see the old fellow pointing toward the girl's room. His wide-eyed glance toward the attic was no more comforting than the shaky finger he was pointing at the girl's door. What's more, he was trying to say something but didn't seem to be able to get it out."

"Birmingham!" shouted Brice. "What is it?" he added as he hurried back down the ladder to see both of his daughters open the door and run inside.

"She's been in there all along, Mr. Brice! She's been in there all along!" he finally managed.

"She?" Brice ran to the open window where his daughters were now standing.

Brice quickly looked out of the window to see what looked to be a woman of Anna's size running like the wind toward the open, barn door. Her pale green gown flowed behind her like something out of a dream. But her face or hair color he couldn't see because of her matching bonnet. Heavy, dark gray clouds darkened the sky as the wet smell of a coming storm presented itself to the mid-day excitement.

"She jumped to the ground from the window, father," said a very excited Anna. She was all the way to the cattle gap before you got to the window. It was Birmingham's ghost."

"I ain't got no ghost," replied Birmingham."

"Ohhh Lord," said Brice weakly as he wheeled around. "Hunter is in the back working on the porch." He wheeled around for another look and saw his son halfway to the cattle gap with Hershey right behind him. "Hunter!" he called loudly, but it never fazed the young boy. "Heather!" he shouted as he ran from the bedroom with everyone right behind him. "Heather!" he repeated desperately as he ran down the stairs. But he got not one answer.

Now through the back door, he could see his wife running toward the cattle gap. She was calling to Hunter also. As

Brice jumped from the porch he spotted his fearless nine-year-old. He was holding to the barn door and peeping inside.

"Go on, Mr. Brice," encouraged Birmingham. "We all be right behind you."

Now the whole, Elmore clan was either at the barn or trying to get through the V-shaped cattle gap. But the fearless Hunter remained reluctant to enter the dark of the barn. He seemed to be jaded by the Lab. Hershey was sneezing and shaking his head as if a bee flew up his nose. That pause gave Heather the time she needed to catch up to her son.

With a firm hold onto the back of his shirt, she peered inside the barn also. "Hello!" she called loudly, but there was not an answer.

"She's in there, Mom," assured Hunter. "I saw her go in. When I got here, she was climbing the ladder to the hay loft. She kind of . . . glowed." He looked back to Birmingham. "I'm not lying, Mr. B. I would have followed her, but the way she laughed didn't sound right."

Birmingham nodded.

"Everyone just stay right here." Brice eased into the barn and then on toward the ladder leading to the loft.

Even though the 'stay here' part was directed at most everyone, Birmingham followed without objection from Brice.

"Mr. Brice?" Birmingham lightly touched his right shoulder. "You sure you want to do this?"

"We'll be fine, Birmingham," whispered Brice. "I just want—"

At that very instant, the shrill laughter came again. This time it was from the hay loft above them. Maniacal it was, and completely void of humor.

"Get out! Get out!" screamed the Green Lady, leaving both Brice and Birmingham frozen in place half way to the ladder.

"Did you hear that?" asked an equally astonished Heather.

"Can't see a thing," added Mrs. Emily from outside the doors. "The outside, loft doors are shut tight."

Birmingham jumped as Hershey sidled up alongside of his right leg. "What makes a sound like that?" he whispered.

Brice slowly shook his head, staring at the opening above the ladder to the hay loft. "If this were a horror movie, I'd say it was a Banshee. But Banshees don't run from people as a rule."

"Brice?" called Heather from the still open barn door.

Brice turned to see her clinging to Hunter as the girls had gathered close to Mrs. Emily.

Brice held up his right hand and then put his index finger across his lips. He then turned and continued toward the ladder.

"My, my," groaned Birmingham as Brice started up the ladder.

Keeping a watchful eye on the lower part of the barn with the occasional glance at those at the door, Birmingham eased up the ladder right behind Brice. He stopped with his head even with the floor of the loft, awaiting Brice's next move.

"Don't say a thing," whispered Brice as he checked the darker corners of the loft with his flashlight.

"Get out! Get out!" came the screams again. But this time they came from below the loft, causing a near panic from those at the door.

Amid the screams of the girls and Heather and Mrs. Emily's shouting and pointing at something on the back side of the barn, Brice could hear Hershey plainly. He was after something and from the growling, he was quite close. All of it was so unsettling, that Birmingham lost his grip and dropped to the floor below.

"She's down here, Mr. Brice," said Birmingham, still on the floor, holding to his right ankle.

"Hurry, Brice," encouraged Heather, now seeing her husband step from the ladder to kneel by Birmingham. "Hershey's had at her and they both left by the back door."

"Go-go," encouraged Birmingham with the wave of his hand. "I'll be jus' fine. Jus' lost a little wind is all."

Brice immediately ran for the still open back door. But as he did, a blinding explosion just passed it all but sent him to the floor of the barn. Shielding his eyes, and now on one knee, Brice hesitated, rubbing his eyes. "Get 'em and get 'em quick!" He could hear Birmingham say, but as he sat back hard on the hay-filled floor, he could hardly see a thing but the brightness still swimming around in his head.

"Are you all right?" asked Heather.

As she knelt by him and tried to wipe his face, he could hear the excitement all around him.

"Forget those outside." He heard Birmingham order. "It's the little ones in here we have to worry about. "I'll check the loft."

"I got the hose," added Mrs. Emily. It's already connected. Jus' show me one and I'll squirt it."

Still trying desperately to see, Brice could only manage the blurry images as they ran to the scattered, glowing images.

"Water over here," said Heather. "Just a little for his face."

Mrs. Emily dribbled a little on Brice's face. The cool of the water quickly soothed his stinging eyes. He could also feel Hershey trying to lick his face. Little by little, he began to see his family scurrying about and checking here and there for little fires.

"Are you all right," asked Birmingham. "Your eyes look really red."

"His whole face is red," added Heather.

"I guess I'm all right." Brice struggled to his feet. "What the devil did I run into?"

"That was her," answered Hunter. "When you and Mr. B tried to chase her, she dropped something just outside the back door. But Hershey got past it before it blew up." He held up a good size piece of the Green Lady's gown. "I think he got a piece of her before she got away."

Mrs. Emily slowly shook her head. "You terrible lucky you weren't any closer to that firecracker when it popped."

"I'm calling the police," said Heather as she helped her husband to his feet. "Someone's going to pay for this nonsense. You could have been badly hurt and we could have lost the whole barn. Someone's definitely going to be arrested."

"Or some thing," said Birmingham. His voice low.

His comment, although weak, garnered a raised eyebrow stare from Heather. "I'd settle for the police right now. This is getting far more serious than I'm comfortable with."

Ω Ω Ω

After the others left for the house, Brice and Birmingham searched behind the barn until he found a clear footprint. It seem to them to be about a size nine —about two sizes smaller than a man would probably wear. Then, as luck would have it, he found a shoe. It was a black one and a perfect size nine. But it fastened with buttons and was no style he was familiar with. Taking it inside the main house, he decided to wait for the Constable. . . .

While they were waiting, Heather sat upon the couch by the window and pondered the shoe. It looked neither old nor brand new, but well taken care of. It was for the right foot and sported five, silver buttons on its right side. There were no button holes, only strong loops.

Anna sat close to her mother, watching closely. "Is that the Green Lady's shoe?" she finally asked.

Heather nodded with a weak "I guess, but this is 1965 and this style was worn a long time ago."

Hailey took the shoe. Looking closely at it, she noted, "But the loops are still on the buttons. How did she lose it?"

"Ha!" came the loud comment from across the room.

All there turned to see Birmingham standing by the shift-a-robe.

"And you were saying?" prompted Brice.

"Jus' makin' an obvious obversation, Mr. Brice. If a ghost could walk through walls, she would have no problem steppin' out o' that shoe. I mean, we heard it scream in the girl's room, but when we got there, it was done clean out o' the house and runnin'."

Brice squinted at the old fellow. "Good point. That still merits some explanation, but I'm still not convinced we're dealing with a gho--"

At that exact instant, someone pulled into the driveway and bumped the siren. Bright white and red lights reflected off of every smooth surface in the living room.

"My, my," groaned Birmingham as he peeped out the nearest front window. "That's got'ta be. . ." He squinted at the well-lit, black Chrysler Newport. "Yep," he finally said. "Nobody but old Andy Devin makes an entrance like that." He threw a quick smile at the others and then added, "The bright lights and noise is supposed to chase trouble away I think." Birmingham stood from the window and looked to Brice. "Mr. Brice, getting' old Andy to catch that Green Lady is like askin' a quail to chase a hawk. Jus' as soon as she pops up, Andy will be flyin' out o' here right behind me." His smile lingered until a rap came upon the front door.

"Birmingham?' Miss Emily briskly walked from the dining area, hitting hard on her heels. "Is your feet glued to the floor?" she asked as she approached the front door. A smile quickly graced her face as she opened it. "Constable Devin," she said happily as she pushed the screen door open. "Come right in. You're jus' the one we need to catch this green haint."

The portly Constable stood there with his eyes frozen on the maid. Well into his fifties and slightly bald, he finally got out, "Awww Mrs. Emily, this place just wears me out. If it ain't voices in the willow trees, things in the closet, crying in the dark, faces in the windows, it's ghosts in the burning Christmas trees. What in the name of Saint Peter is happening now?" The Constable slowly looked up to the porch ceiling. "Sky blue," he finally got out. "Is this for bugs or--"

"Haints," replied Mrs. Emily, still holding the door open. "Come on in. We got us a problem that'll just suit you."

Andy stepped inside, eying Birmingham. The grin upon his face looked glued in place.

"Don't worry about this spook stuff," said Brice. "We're having a problem with a burglar. "We just chased her from the house and into the barn. When we got there, we must have got too close. She caused something to explode and Brice caught the worst of it."

"Yes," agreed Heather. "It almost got him and showered sparks all over the barn and into the stalls. Just take a look at his face."

"Little fires popped up everywhere," added Anna.

"And it was green," said Birmingham.

"The fires were green? Andy squinted at Birmingham.

"No, Andy." Mrs. Heather held out a two-foot long piece of the Green Lady's gown. "Out interloper glowed green. Hershey got a piece of her before she got away.

Brice handed him the shoe. "She left this behind also. It's a size nine."

"Surely you don't expect me to go pokin' around outside this place tonight do you? My flashlight batteries are almost dead." He slowly looked to Heather and then back to Brice. "This ain't some kind of joke is it? I know this old house has a sizable reputation, but I was told you folks tamed it down a bit."

"We still got something," grumbled Brice. "What it is and what it's trying to tell us is the problem right now. Every time one of us gets too close to it, she screams 'Get Out!'."

"And it glows?" Andy squinted at the piece of gown in his hand.

At that instant the living room lights went out.

"Damn!" exclaimed Andy as the glowing piece of garment floated to the floor.

Instantly, the lights were back on.

Mrs. Emily, standing by the switch at the front door, smiled at the big officer. "Does that solve that riddle for you?"

"Just check around the house for us, Andy," suggested Brice. "I've got an old, double barrel sixteen gauge shotgun hanging on the wall over the fireplace. This is our home and I take extreme exception to anything or anyone trying to drive us away from it."

"My word," groaned the Constable, scratching his head under his beige, western hat. "Halloween's comin' in with a bang around here ain't it?"

"Yep," agreed Birmingham. "And it got a curious shade o' green."

Ω   Ω   Ω

But the Green Lady of Weeping Willows didn't sleep that night either. Constable Andy Devin moved his car into the yard to where he could see the front, the north side of the house, and the barn beyond it as well. But calm in this chilly but hopefully peaceful night was about to hit the fan again. . . .

Well after 8:00PM, Andy sat in his patrol car listening to the quiet hum of the Chrysler's heater. Resting his head back on the headrest, he closed his eyes as he listened to his Neal Diamond cassette on the eight track.

"Andy?" spoke a soft voice along with a slight tap on his window.

Andy jumped. "What? What?" The Constable quickly sat up, noticing Heather holding a brown bag and a green thermos. "We are just about to eat a little something and thought that you might be hungry as well. It's almost nine. It isn't too late for you is it?"

The slight grease stains on the bag spelt relief for him. "Ohhh, no, Ma'am." Andy quickly rolled down the window, smelling the onions and beef on the hamburger.

Heather smiled, handing him the bag and thermos. "There's some French fries in there as well as coffee in the thermos. I remember you like it black."

"Yes, Ma'am. Thank you, Ma'am," replied Andy with a smile. "This is very kind of you. I'll stay here 'till midnight and on into the morning if needs be."

"Midnight will be fine, Andy," said Heather. She turned and headed back toward the house.

Andy immediately opened the sack. The aroma of fresh beef, onions, and mustard was like a piece of Heaven for the big man. Pulling the wax paper wrapped treat from the bag, he stared at what looked to be a large order of steak fries.

"Fantastic," he said with a smile.

Half a large cheeseburger and eight fries later, the Constable heard something outside, but could make no sense of who would be laughing at this time of night. Checking toward the barn, the mirrors, and each side of the car, he could see no one at all. Then, in the middle of the next bite of hamburger, he got a glimpse of something floating through the cattle cap. It was glowing an eerie shade of green and heading straight for his car. All of a sudden, and as if in a bad dream, the 'whoever' launched a basketball-sized pumpkin at the patrol vehicle.

"What!" exclaimed the Constable.

Andy dropped his hamburger to the seat on his right and grabbed the shift lever. But it was to no avail." The pumpkin exploded on the windshield sending pieces flying everywhere.

"Damn! Damn!" he exclaimed as he shoved the door open, scrambled out of the vehicle, and pulled his revolver.

Pointing the Smith and Wesson toward the barn and then the darkness each side of the patrol car, he couldn't find nothing at all.

"Andy!" spoke someone loudly from the Elmore's front porch, all of sixty feet from where he was standing.

"Mr. Brice!" answered Andy loudly. "Somethin's had at me."

Brice trotted from the porch with Birmingham and Heather right behind him.

"Great Gods," replied Brice, seeing the pumpkin pieces lying on the car as well as all around in the grass. "Looks like they got you, Andy. Are you all right?"

Andy slowly shook his head as he holstered his pistol. "No Sir, I ain't. At least not until I put a permanent limp into the person that is doing this to us."

"Wait a minute," said Brice. "I got a hose on the side of the house. I believe it'll reach your car.

But just as soon as Brice turned on the water hose, Anna ran out of the house and onto the front porch. "Come quick!" she exclaimed. "Hunter just came in the back door and there's blood all over his hands and pants. Dad, he's crying so much he can hardly talk."

"I got this." Birmingham grabbed the hose as Brice turned and ran with his wife and the Constable for porch steps.

"He's in the bath room," explained Anna as they ran through the living room. "Mrs. Emily and Hailey have him sitting on the floor. He's so weak he can hardly stand."

"Ohhh my God," said Heather. She pushed by Brice and took the lead through the dining room.

As they approached the bathroom, they could see Hailey standing at the doorway. Clearly shaken, she managed, "Something shook him up real bad, Dad, but we don't think he's hurt."

Heather stopped, looking down at her son with Mrs. Emily kneeling in the floor beside him. "But the blood," said Heather. "There's so much blood."

"Not his," explained Mrs. Emily as Birmingham ran up behind those at the doorway. "He keep sayin' somethin' 'bout Hershey in the barn," she explained.

"She hit him, Dad," sobbed Hunter. "The green ghost hit him bad."

Brice wheeled, glanced at Andy, and then pushed by them all for the living room with Birmingham right behind him.

"Everybody just stay right here and don't go outside," ordered Andy. "I'll be with them."

When the Constable ran into the living room, he spotted Brice at the fireplace. He had loaded the double and was putting more Super X shells into this pocket. He glanced at Andy. "Birmingham's getting the one-mile light. Let's go and find Hershey."

Part 3
Fire with Fire

Now, with his temper heated to the point of flame, Brice stepped from the front porch with Andy and Birmingham right behind him. On through the cattle gap they went with Birmingham directing the powerful one-mile's beam toward the barn doors.

"Mr. Brice?" Birmingham tugged on the back of Brice's jacket stopping him.

The grey, wintry clouds hung low and heavy with no sign of a moon. But, dark as it was, Brice could see what Birmingham's light was directed at. Barely fifteen feet in front of the barn doors lay Hershey. Bright, wet-looking red against chocolate brown stood out like a full moon on a clear night.

"Lord All Mighty. . ." Brice instantly handed the Bellmore to Birmingham and ran the short distance to the Lab.

With his head lying in a pool of blood, his eyes were closed, and he was not moving at all. A cotton chopping hoe was lying just inside the barn doorway, stained with the same color as was on Hershey's dark brown coat.

Dropping to his right knee, Brice quickly scooped up the one he had raised from a bottle and started back toward the cattle gap. "Run to the house," he pleaded to Birmingham. "Get Heather to call old Doc Rhea. I don't know a vet well enough ask for help at this hour but I think old Doc will be happy to do so."

"Yes Sir Mr. Brice," answered the old handy man as he ran past them. "I'll warm up the car too."

So, off Birmingham ran, seemingly racing Brice toward the house. Glancing back, he could see the huge Lab draped lifelessly over Brice's arms with a huge piece of skin peeled back from his ears, almost covering his eyes. He still wasn't moving.

♎   ♎   ♎

Shortly after 10:00PM, Birmingham raced northwest on Highway thirty-five toward Doc Rhea's home with Brice holding Hershey in the back seat. Hunter was holding a white towel against the wound. Quickly pulling the white Impala into Doc's drive, all could see that not only every light was on in the house.

A lady, short blond hair and in her mid-fifties, stepped onto the porch as they got out of the car. "Is he alive?" she asked.

Brice shrugged, glancing at his son. Trying to hold a towel over the Lab's head, they walked briskly toward the porch.

"Ohhh my," she added. "Bring him in quickly. Sis Gordin is on her way here from the veterinarian's here at Vaiden," she added as she held the screen door open for them.

"Doc's nurse?" asked Brice as he entered the house.

"The same." She pointed to a hallway on their left. "Down the hall, Brice. Last room on the end. Lay him on the covered table and take a seat." She stepped close to Hershey and gently lifted the towel. "He's stopped bleeding and he's gonna need a lot of stitches."

Once in the room, Brice did as he was instructed and then took a seat with Hunter and Birmingham.

Birmingham looked at a nearby tray. It was loaded with steaming water, bandages, antiseptic, and a dozen or so chrome instruments. Almost immediately, Doc Rhea entered the room with his wife, Becky and went straight to Hershey.

Hunter, wiping his eyes, looked at his father. "Why did she hurt Hershey? Are there good ghosts as well as bad ones?"

"Ghosts?" Doc Rhea looked up from the wound with his steaming rag. "Are you still having problems at Weeping Willows?" He glanced at Hunter. "Whoever did this to your dog is no ghost, son."

Brice nodded. "That's my opinion also. But the reason for these encounters still has me baffled. I think Hershey got a little too close to our supposed spook."

"The Green Lady," grumbled Hunter.

The old doctor glanced at Brice. "Some kind of Halloween prank gone bad?"

"More criminal now," added Becky.

"We'll get to the bottom of it," assured Brice. "This just got very personal."

♎   ♎   ♎

Most of that night was troublesome for the Elmore household, especially for Hunter. The old doc's diagnosis was fifty-fifty at best. Hershey had a concussion and had lost what Doc had described as "an alarming amount of blood" so he kept the family pet overnight to keep a close eye on him. But the most fearless member of the Elmore clan woke early the next morning as the sun just started coloring the eastern sky. With an anger that was still kindled to the point of flame, Hunter formulated his own demise for the Green Lady of Weeping Willows. It was time to fight fire with fire and the lad knew just where to go and get the flame he needed. . . .

Hunter eased from his bedroom and peeped into the living room. It was still mostly dark and not a sound could he heard. He knew it was Saturday and everyone would, most likely, be slow to get up. He paused, listening to the old grandfather clock strike six. But this was no time to sleep. Still in his jeans, he opted for a jacket, slipped his tennis shoes on without sox, and then crept on toward the front door. His father's snoring was the perfect camouflage for the noise the deadbolt was about to make. Gaining the front porch, he eased on out onto the steps. The skies were remarkably clear and the half-moon's glow presented the barn's front lot with a yellow hue. Off he went, barely pausing to sidle through the cattle gap, he paused to check out the barn. He knew full well that if he ran across the Green Lady, he would come out just like Hershey or worse. But thinking that his adversary had done her damage for a while, he headed for the smaller, side door of the barn. It led to the tack room and from there, he knew he could check out the main part of the barn before making a move there. Once in the tack room, and with the help of the moon's light through the windows, he found one of six oil lanterns that still had a goodly amount of oil left. He knew it was totally dark in the main part of the barn and to him, that was unacceptable. Quickly finding the match tin, he carefully lit the wick and turned down the flame until the light was bright and the glass chimney wouldn't soot up. As he eased out of the tack room and into the more open part of the barn, he remembered his father warning about carrying the lantern around. Immediately placing it on one of several lantern hooks, he then turned toward the three stalls on the far side. Seeing not a thing but hay, his gaze ended up on the huge tack chest to the right of the tack room door.

"Susan. . ." he whispered, knowing full well that was the place she first met Hershey. "Susan!" he called again.

Silence.

"Susan! Susan! Susan!" he shouted again and again.

Still. . .nothing.

Tears welled up in his eyes as he climbed atop the big, wooden and brass box and sat down, facing the stalls on the far side. "She hurt Hershey! The mean ghost hurt Hershey and he may die." He wiped his wet face with the sleeve of his jacket. "You love him as much as we do and he loved you too. I need your help. We all need your help."

Hunter looked all about the dimly lit barn as he listened to a rooster crow in the distance. Silently he sat there, feeling his tears slide down his cheeks to the underside of his chin. Afraid he would miss his one-time friend in her yellow buttercup dress, he leaned back against the wall and listened to the roosters call as he dozed. Then, in total darkness, he saw Susan's face. The little, blue-eyed blond was smiling at him.

"Been here long?" she said softly.

Slowly looking about the darkness, he could see not a thing past her face. The soft glow of the oil lamp was no longer there. But he could still feel the chest he was sitting on.

"Where are we?" he whispered.

"Neither here nor there," she answered smiling.

"Grandfather said something was very wrong and there was a need."

"A need?" Hunter squinted. "Is that why you came?"

"I didn't come, Hunter. You came to me," she answered with a most confident smile. "Just as soon as you sat upon this chest, I knew your problem. I am told Hershey still lives, but is struggling."

"Then. . ." Hunter squinted. "You know of the Green Lady?"

"I know not of her, Hunter. She is not from here. You must be very careful. Whoever is taunting you is driven either by He who is dark or by greed which can be just as bad sometimes."

"But can't you help us?" asked Hunter.

"Possible," she answered with a smile. "But one just can't alter the natural course of events on a whim. There must be a need."

"A need?"

Hunter watched as her face began to disappear. It was as though the slow return of the lanterns light was driving her away somehow.

"We have a need!" exclaimed Hunter as he watched the face fade, seemingly into the light of the lantern. "The Green Lady wants us out of our home. She wants our home for herself."

"You have said, Hunter Elmore," came the voice from the darkness of the far side of the barn. "Think on that," added the little ghost and then there was silence.

At that moment, something very large came rushing toward him, striking his whole, left side. Groaning, and holding to his now sore head, Hunter rolled to his back and looked across the barn floor toward a light at the front doors.

"Hunter, is you in there?"

"Mr. B. . ." Hunter scrambled to a sitting position and looked toward the old handyman holding one of the big doors open.

Birmingham quickly walked toward the youngster, took the oil lamp from the hook, and then blew it out. "I saw this shinin' through the window from the kitchen in the main house. Have you taken complete leave of your senses? With everything goin' on 'round here, you shouldn' be out here by yourself. If Mr. Brice knew you were in here with his old lamp, he apt to be loosin' his mind too and in your direction. Now, let's get out of here right now."

"Yes, Sir, Mr. B," said Hunter as he stood, brushing himself off.

Birmingham put the lamp back on the hook and looked down at

Hunter. "You been sleepin' out here?"

"No Sir, Mr. B. I was just looking for help to catch that Green Lady."

"Help how?" Birmingham squinted. "You the onliest somebody out here."

"This is where I first met Susan."

"Susan?" The old handyman's squint was back. He slowly ran his fingers over what little short, black hair he had left.

"It's time to fight fire with fire, Mr. B. If anyone can catch that green spook I know she can. After all, look what she done to that bully Molly Hatchet. I'll bet Molly still has nightmares about getting her hair all tied up in the girl's closet."

"Uh huh," replied Birmingham weakly. "And did you see her again?"

Hunter shrugged. "Not sure, Mr. B. I dozed off on the top of the chest. I did dream of her though. I think she said she might be able to help us." He frowned, brushing his pants off again. "But I fell off the chest and woke up. That's when you came in."

"Well, it's close to seven right now and your folks gonna be sturrin' soon. Mrs. Emily got ham in the pan and biscuits 'bout ready to go in the stove. Come with me and we'll get us a bite before the rest are up. We'll jus' keep this mornin' barn adventure to ourselves for now. If your mom finds out you were in the barn at this hour, she'll have a conniption."

Entering the back door of the old farm house, Hunter could see Mrs. Emily in the kitchen, fussing about the stove. Anna and Hailey, however, were both already seated at the table, eying him suspiciously. The half-grin upon their faces instantly proved troublesome. He knew explanations were in order. But he thought they might be more understanding than anyone else in the family.

"Right here," said Anna, pointing to his chair at the table. "We saw Mr. B bring you out of the barn." She looked closely at him. "Your face is dusty. There are tear tracks all over it."

"Why were you crying?" asked Hailey.

Hunter quickly checked the kitchen, wiping his face again. Both Mr. B and Mrs. Emily were busy at the stove.

"I was begging for help," he whispered. He leaned closer to his sisters. "It's time to fight fire with fire," he explained, rubbing his red eyes.

Both girls squinted.

"I'm lost," admitted Anna as Hailey slowly nodded.

"I went into the barn this morning at first light," explained Hunter. "That's where I first met Susan. I begged for her to come back and help us."

Both sisters leaned closer. "And. . ." they chimed together.

"Well. . ." Hunter checked the kitchen again. "She didn't come--at least like we saw her before. Guess I fell asleep, 'cause I saw her in a dream I think. She said she might help us, but I woke up before she could explain how."

Both sisters sat back, looking at their brother.

"So now what's gonna happen?" asked Hailey.

Hunter shrugged. "If Susan comes, maybe we'll know what to do."

Ω   Ω   Ω

Not long after breakfast, around 9:30AM or so, a call came in to the Elmore house. Everyone in the living room watched Birmingham as he promptly answered the phone. The smile slowly forming on his face was the first sign of hope that day. . . .

Hanging up the wall-mounted phone, Birmingham looked all about the dining room and on into the living room. His gaze ended up on the girls, sitting on the couch by the window with Hunter.

"Mr. B!" said Hailey loudly. "You're killing us. Was that the doctor?"

Birmingham slowly nodded. "Hershey's fine. He's all sewed up and even eating Doctor Rhea said. Can't explain the quick recovery though. Said the wound, although big, might not have been as bad as it looked." His smile widened. "Also said we could come and get 'em."

Hunter and his sisters jumped from the couch, cheering and laughing.

Ω Ω Ω

Thirty minutes later, a white, 1959 Impala pulled into the driveway of the old doctor's home. Brice and Heather got out of the front seat to be joined by Hunter, Hailey and Anna from the back.

"Got room for Hershey back there?" poked Heather.

"We'll manage," answered Hailey. "Let's just get him out first."

Ω Ω Ω

At approximately 11:00AM that morning, the Elmore family got their four-legged member back home. That afternoon, he remained a bit reserved. Not once did he ask out. In front of the couch where Hunter was sitting quickly became his favorite spot. The Saturday night movie garnered just about everyone's attention. Even Mrs. Emily and Birmingham liked Tarzan, and 'The Ape Man' was their favorite. At 10:00PM, Hunter dodged the evening news and retired to his room with Hershey right behind him.

Anna watched the two until Hunter closed the door. "Well. . ." She paused, smiling. "I think he's after the fire place in Hunter's room."

Hailey nodded. "Probably too much of an effort to climb the stairs to ours where he usually sleeps."

Ω Ω Ω

That night, well after the news had ended, Hunter was awaken by a soft woof at the foot of his bed.

Slowly sitting up, he spotted Hershey's silhouette in the glow of the fireplace that he shared with his parents in the adjoining bedroom. The big Chocolate Labrador was sitting up and looking at the partially open bedroom door.

"Woof. . ." The breathy warning of abnormality came again.

The nine-year-old eased his feet from the quilts onto the cold, hardwood floor and looked for Hershey. He seemed to be waiting for him at the door with his nose well into the six inch opening. Hunter eased up behind him, gently touched his back, and then peeped into the dark living room. But as soon as he did, Hershey nosed through the doorway, trotted into the living room and then on to the dining area. The barefooted Hunter, trying to be as quiet as possible, followed him through the dining area and then toward the stairs on the right side. Once at the head of the stairs, Hershey paused to look back at

Hunter. But just as soon as Hunter caught up, he trotted along the bannisters toward the girl's bedroom. Hunter's mouth ran dry as the Lab passed his sister's bedroom and continued the short distance to the storage room. Pausing at the door, he sat down and looked back at Hunter.

"Not this soon again," whispered Hunter as he eased up to the door and listened.

Someone was moving about on the other side of the doorway—not in the room as it were, but seemingly above it somehow.

"Easy, Hershey," whispered Hunter, noting the Lab's ears perked toward the door.

Hunter got a good grip on Hershey's collar and then slowly opened the door. But when he did, the big Labrador exploded. Jerking from Hunter's hand, he charged into the room barking and growling. With wide-eyed disbelief, the youngest member of the Elmore clan froze, staring at the Green Lady half in and half out of the only window in the room.

"Sick 'em Hershey," screamed Hunter, seeing the green spook's left leg was still in play.

Now, the screaming was coming from the Green Lady as well as Hunter's two sisters in the adjoining bedroom. Hunter stood his ground just inside the doorway and watched the struggle at the window.

"What's happening!" shouted Hailey as she and Anna ran into the hallway.

But the slamming of the storage room window marked the exit of the ghost leaving Hershey with a mouth full of blood-stained green gown.

Now, every light was on in the main house. Hearing someone running up the stairs, all three kids looked down from the bannisters.

"What the devil's going on up here?" exclaimed Brice as he topped the stairway with Heather right behind him.

"It's her again," replied a much excited Hinter, shaking a finger at the storage room doorway.

Hershey sat there, bandaged head and all, looking pleased as peas with his mouth full of the spook's green, blood-stained garment.

"He got her good, Dad," said Hunter, pulling the garment from the Lab. "She got her real good. She heard the ghost all the way from my room downstairs."

Brice looked at the material in his son's right hand and then at his daughters. The look on their faces was a mixture of shock, disbelief, and horror.

"A ghost doesn't bleed," said Brice as he walked by his son, patted Hershey's shoulders, and then continued on into the storage room and turned on the overhead light.

Hunter stepped in right behind his father and pointed up to the ceiling just above the doorway. The ceiling in that room was designed with three-foot square panels. The adjoining seams between each panel made it easy to hide the other door that now had been left ajar by the hasty retreat of their goblin.

"She left it like that, Dad," said Hunter. "She was trying to get in the attic or maybe leave the house when we caught her."

Brice walked briskly to the window, opened it, and then looked about the front yard. "Well. . ." He eased back inside and lowered the window. "It's almost midnight and we'll never catch him or her out there right now."

Then, noticing something underfoot at the base of the window, he reached down and picked it up.

"A shoe?" asked Heather.

"A bloody shoe," corrected Brice. He looked at Hunter. "I think you're right, son. He did get her good."

"Shouldn't we call Officer Jackson?" asked Heather. "I know it's late, but I don't think I can go back to sleep right now."

Brice looked at the others. All were silently shaking their heads.

"Well, I'll have the Constable to either come or have someone sent to look about the place and check it occasionally tonight for us."

"Wait a minute," said Heather.

Taking the shoe, she looked at it closely and then removed a piece of folded paper from inside. Trying to dodge the blood stains, she carefully unfolded the paper.

"Well?" prompted Brice, seeing she seemed puzzled.

"Can't make sense of it," grumbled Heather. "Oenothera it is written, like a heading. It says 'Start at noon then one and four.'" She squinted, looking up at Brice. "What does that mean?"

Brice shrugged, glancing at the others.

"What's an Oenothera?" asked Hunter

"I have no idea," admitted Brice. He smiled, looking at his daughters. "I think this is a job for our young detectives. You two solved little Susan's problem." Give them the paper and let them work on this."

"Agreed," replied Heather, handing her daughters the 'shoe note'.

"Four detectives," corrected Hunter.

"Very well," laughed Brice. "I'll call the Constable and everyone else back to bed.

"We're sleeping on a pallet with Hershey," said Hailey, glancing at her sister."

"Sounds good to me," agreed Anna. "There's no telling how many more trap doors are in this place."

"Everyone make sure their windows are locked." Brice looked to Hunter. "If Hershey sounds the alarm again, you come and get me right away. I'll have Old Betsy at the head of the bed. We'll give that would be ghost a taste of number nine birdshot for its troubles."

Ω   Ω   Ω

Fifteen minutes later, Hunter sat upon his bed listening to the girls walk down the stairway and toward his room. Hershey had already curled up at the fireplace and looked to be sound asleep. But there was something different. Somehow, the oak scent from the firewood had changed.

Anna eased the door open with a slight knock. "Can we come in?"

Hunter got up and straightened the bed covers. "You two take the bed. I'll sleep on a pallet next to Hershey." He paused, slowly looking about the bedroom.

"What's the matter?" asked Hailey. "You look worried or something."

Without a word, Hunter walked to the far side of his bed, sniffing the air. Stopping at the window, he turned and faced his sisters. "Do you smell something different?"

"Yes," replied Anna. "As a matter of fact I do."

"It's honeysuckle," added Hailey. "But it's October and honeysuckle isn't blooming right now."

Hunter eased toward a now awake Hershey and paused at the foot of his bed. The big, Chocolate Labrador was staring right at him. Hunter noticed the strange glow in his eyes. It seemed to be reflecting the . . .

"Wait a minute," said Hunter. He stepped closer to Hershey, looking carefully at his eyes.

"Ohhh my God," groaned Anna. "They're glowing aren't they. Let's get--"

"Don't bother Dad," said Hunter. "He's had enough for one night." Hunter knelt on his right knee, again looking closely at Hershey. "Susan?"

Anna and Hailey's mouth opened slightly, but each said not a word as they watched the Lab's ears perk up with a breathy but soft woof.

Hunter slowly scooted away until his back was against the footboard. "So. . . You are going to help us. No wonder Hershey got well so quick."

Part 4
Secret of the Primrose

Halloween came in with a bang for the Elmore clan and all were up bright and early that Sunday morning. Church was on their mind, but that was a luxury to them. The business of the day had to be handled and all knew that Andy, or someone from the Sheriff's department would be there shortly. But, as Fate would dictate, Halloween was long from over. . . .

Mrs. Emily hustled about the kitchen while Birmingham poured the coffee and served the fresh biscuits. But just when he and Mrs. Emily sat down to join the others, a rather loud knock sounded at the screen door on the front porch.

"I got it," replied Anna, holding Mr. B to his chair.

Taking a quick bite of sausage and biscuit, she trotted into the living room, stopping at the front door to peek through the window.

She quickly looked back at her father. "It's Mrs. Crutcher," she said, squinting.

"What?" Brice slowly stood. "Well. . ." He glanced at Heather. "Let her in, Anna."

The eighteen-year-old reluctantly opened the front door, stepped out onto the screened in front porch, and then unlatched its screen door. "Why Mrs. Crutcher, what brings you here on a Sunday?" Anna's voice low.

"Child. . ." Mrs. Crutcher leaned to her right, looking past the front door and into the house. "I would like a word with your parents."

Anna backed away, still holding the door open. "Come in. The Family's at the breakfast table."

By now, Brice and Heather were standing at the entrance way to the living room as Mrs. Crutcher walked inside.

"What can we do for you, Mrs. Crutcher?" asked Brice.

She glanced nervously past Brice and Heather to those still at the table.

"I apologize. It was not my intention to disturb your breakfast."

"That's not a problem, Mrs. Crutcher," replied Brice. "May we offer you something to eat? We have plenty."

"Ohhh no, Mr. Elmore," replied Mrs. Crutcher, still seemingly nervous. Forcing a smile, she looked at Hershey as he sat down beside Heather, looking at her intently.

"My daughter knows Dr. Rhea's wife and she said an intruder tried to kill your dog. She said you all called the intruder the Green Lady."

"Yes," replied Brice. "We're having a little trouble with trespassers but we're working on that right now."

"I see." She glanced at an unusually quiet Heather and then looked back to Brice. "I feel dreadful about selling you this old house and all. I knew others before you had their troubles with it, what with their over active imaginations and all. Now, this Green Lady thing comes along and seems to lend credence to what they went through."

"Strange isn't it?" asked Heather, breaking her silence. "You weren't totally honest with us at first. But, all in all, things worked out for the best for us anyway."

"For the best?" Mrs. Crutcher squinted. "I was told that Mrs. Jackie Christopher was scared to death right here in this very room not long ago. How does 'for the best' work into it?"

"That's a lie," snapped Birmingham. He dropped his linen napkin to his plate and stood. "We were there when she passed. Her loved ones were all around her when she did."

Glaring indignantly at the old handyman, Mrs. Crutcher grumbled, "I was speaking to the Elmore family, not their hired help."

"He is family," spoke Anna loudly. "Both him and Mrs. Emily are family."

"Yes, well. . ." Mrs. Crutcher checked those at the table again. All were standing and not a soul was eating. "It just bothered me that you all were stuck with this old, drafty house what with the ghosts and such. I thought I'd give you a chance to get your investment back."

"We're fine, Mrs. Crutcher," replied Brice. "This is our home and we'll defend it as much as needs be."

"Well. . ." she replied through a breathy sigh. Noting the smiling faces, she added, "If you should change your mind, you know where to find me." She then turned, but paused at the door. Looking back at Brice, she added, "I have an offer for that old, grandfather clock Mr. Christopher made."

"Not interested," spoke Brice instantly.

"I see." Without another word, Mrs. Crutcher left the house hitting heavily on her heels.

Anna got up, and slowly walked toward the still open front door. After Mrs. Crutcher stepped from the front porch, she turned toward her father. "That's totally weird."

"It's perfect," corrected Hunter, smiling broadly. "Halloween's just started and we've already had a visit from the wicked witch of the west."

"Hunter!" Heather squinted at her son while Brice turned away smiling.

Ω Ω Ω

Later that morning, as most of the Elmore's attended church, Birmingham prepared the outdoor, brick bar-b-que for the family Halloween party. He and Mrs. Emily took the day away from their church because of Mrs. Emily's head cold. Hunter, with the same affliction, had planted himself on the living room couch with Hershey and was watching the movie, 'Lassie Come Home'. . . .

"Hamburgers?" queried Birmingham, glancing at Mrs. Emily, just inside the back, screen door.

"And smoke sausage," she replied proudly. "Jus' made 'em at the market—extra lean. That's the way Mr. Brice likes 'em. Be right back," she added walking away from the back door. In less than a minute, she trotted right back. "Who do we know that drives and old, white Dodge truck?"

Birmingham looked back from the grill, squinting. Sitting down his bag of charcoal, he joined his wife in the house and they both headed for the front door. Noting Hershey was already there, he took hold of his collar and opened it. In their mid-twenties, a pleasant looking young couple stood there smiling.

"If you're lookin' for the Elmore's, they're at church," replied Birmingham. "Perhaps I can help you."

"We don't really need them," replied the read-headed fellow as he gently tugged at the latched, screen door. Holding up a piece of paper, he added, "I am James Smith and this is my wife, Judy. I have a paper signed by Mr. Brice Elmore that says I can pick up an old, grandfather clock made by the original owner, a

Mr. Clarence Christopher."

Birmingham looked back at Mrs. Emily. She was slowly shaking her head.

"Come here, boy," called Hunter to Hershey.

Birmingham turned loose of the Lab's collar to let the dog join his master. "My, my. . ." Birmingham slowly looked back at James. "I 'spect you best come back in a couple o' hours and see Mr. Brice 'bout that. He's the one who--"

All of a sudden, and with no warning at all, James jerked the screen door open, sending his chrome hook bouncing across the porch floor, stopping at Birmingham's feet. The old handyman froze, looking at the chrome automatic the young man's right hand.

"Be careful with that thing, mister," said Birmingham as he raised his hands and backed away from the front door.

"Hunter, hold that dog," said Mrs. Emily, noting that James was looking at him intently.

But strangely, the big, Chocolate Labrador made no attempt to leave the couch. He seemed satisfied to just watch the goings on beside Hunter.

James chuckled softly. "Not much of a guard dog is he?" he said, smiling at Hunter.

Hunter shrugged, still holding tightly to the lab's collar. "She's just watching for now."

"She?" The blond-haired girl stood there smiling at the boy on the couch. "The dog's a male, little boy."

"Yep," replied Hunter, grinning. "The dog is."

Judy squinted, but only shook her head.

"Mr. B?" Mrs. Emily stepped from the dining room doorway. I got a cake in the oven I need to check." Her eyes were glued to James' pistol.

"Make it fast," said Judy. "I'll be watching." She turned to look at the old clock. "You didn't tell me it was this big," she said, walking toward the clock. "It's over a foot taller than I am."

"Go sit on the couch," ordered James to Birmingham. "The woman will join you in a minute."

But as Judy reached out to touch the carved flower below its face, she froze with her eyes tightly shut and then slowly sank to her knees. Birmingham quickly stood.

"Sit back down!" snapped James.

"Please put that thing up," begged Birmingham. "Everyone here's either too young or too old to put up a fuss."

Seeing Judy still on her knees at the base of the old clock, James quickly put the pistol back in his jacket pocket and rushed over to help her.

"I saw him,' she said weakly as she pushed herself away from the old timepiece. "Get out!" he shouted-- just like I told the other Elmores."

Hunter immediately sat up smiling. "So you're the Green Lady. She's the only one who's been telling us to get out. Dad was right. There is no ghost." Hunter smiled, noticing the bandage on Judy's left ankle. "I see Hershey left his mark on you didn't he?"

Both Judy and James glared at the little boy, but seeing the big Labrador was still staring at them, they did nothing.

"Judy. . ." James squinted at Hershey. "There's something funny about his eyes." He reached down and helped Judy to her feet adding, "It won't take long. Just help me get the clock out to the truck."

"I'm not touching that thing," replied Judy, now looking at Hershey also. She pulled her stare from the Lab and looked at James. "You can check it right here and right now."

James rolled his eyes. "You lost the paper. Remember? I can't remember what the old man wrote."

Judy rolled her eyes, glancing at Hershey again. "I read it also. It was something like start at noon. Then it mentioned something about one and four or two and three or whatever."

"That's just great," grumbled James, as he turned toward the old clock.

But when he did, he noticed that Hershey and moved from beside Hunter on the couch and was now sitting at the base of the timepiece. Seeing that, he instantly looked back to the couch and Hunter. The young boy was sitting there with the unbuckled collar in his right hand.

Quickly realizing he no longer had Hershey, Hunter quickly shook his head. "I didn't do it. I didn't do it," he exclaimed. "It just slipped off somehow."

Hunter immediately jumped from the couch toward the Labrador. But when he did, he seemingly fell back to where he was sitting. Quickly regaining his feet, he was about to try again when he froze dead still on the left side of the coffee table. His eyes grew wide and transfixed on something smoking and hovering about two feet in front of James' face.

"The Grandfather's pipe," said Hunter weakly.

James, now with his stare fixed on the old, smoking briarwood, slowly eased his hand to the right side of his jacket. But his hand stopped right above the pocket when a match seemingly lit itself right above the bowl of the old pipe.

"That's it!" said Judy weakly. She wheeled and ran for the front door. But as she did, she noticed a little, blond-haired girl in a yellow, buttercup dress holding it open for her. Not missing a step, and not wanting to make eye contact with the little girl, Judy ran from the house, across the porch, and hardly checked up for the screen door. Although James turned to watch, it seemed that Fate had refused to let his hand move any closer to the pistol in his pocket. Feeling the warm tobacco smoke now swirling about in front of his face, he slowly turned back to the floating pipe.

Birmingham's eyes grew big as the match's flame was again drawn down into the tobacco. But neither he nor Mrs. Emily, Hunter or Hershey moved from where they were. Little by little, the match's flame revealed the wire-rimmed glasses, the crystal blue eyes, and then the smiling face of Mr. Clarence Christopher floating behind the pipe and flame. His eyes sparkled with delight as he noted the horrified expression upon James' face.

"Mr. Crutcher. . ." said Clarence calmly. "Lay not a hand upon my clock. If you trouble this house again or the family therein, I will show you the meaning of haunted."

Pulling his hand away from his jacket pocket, James slowly backed toward the front door. Stumbling over and then sitting down upon the boot and hat rack there, he quickly looked toward the little girl still holding the door open.

"Watch your step," she said, smiling at him broadly.

Then, as if someone had stuck him with a cattle prod, James bounced from the boot and hat rack, ran from the room, and all but took the porch screen door off its hinges.

"Miss. Judy done left and took the truck," noted Mrs. Emily as she looked toward the window behind the couch on the far side of the coffee table.

Ain't botherin' him none," noted Birmingham, also looking out of the window. "He just turned right and headed toward Munford. Never slowed down at all."

"The Grandfather and Susan are gone," said Hunter, causing both Mrs. Emily and Birmingham to turn from the window.

"Yep." Birmingham smiled, looking at the pipe smoke still hanging in the air. "Somehow, I think as long as that old clock is here, Mr. Clarence won't be far from us."

"They wanted the clock," noted Mrs. Emily. "But I don't think it would hold much value to anyone but. . ." Her voice trailed off, leaving her squinting at Birmingham. "Say, Mr. Clarence called that James follow Mr. Crutcher didn't he?"

Both Birmingham and Hunter nodded, watching the pipe smoke slowly disappear.

"The girls have that shoe note from Mr. Christopher don't they?" asked Birmingham.

"They do," answered Mrs. Emily. "I think they found it upstairs somewhere after that Green Lady spook left. That old clock's got somethin' in it they wanted in a bad way," added Mrs. Emily.

"Yep." Birmingham stared down at the gold, Double Eagle he had just taken from his pocket. "It's jus' 'bout time for church to let out. Maybe when Mr. Brice and all get here, we can make some sense out o' all this."

"Yes," added Mrs. Emily, "and have him call Munford Police and tell 'em we jus' had burglars from the Crutcher family again."

Ω Ω Ω

Shortly after noon, Brice and family pulled into the driveway from church. Hunter, immediately spotting them, ran from the house with Hershey right behind him. The latter now acting like himself as he bounced around trying to entice a little play from Hunter. . . .

"They were here again? The Green Lady was here and now we know who she is!" he exclaimed, stopping just short of Brice as he got out.

"Calm down. Calm down," said Brice. "Who is 'they', how do you know who the Green Lady is, and where are 'they' now?" He glanced up the walkway at Mrs. Emily and Birmingham on the front porch steps.

"James and Judy Smith," answered Hunter. "They were here to pick up the Grandfather's old clock but Mr. Christopher and Susan stopped them."

Brice, now joined by the rest of the family, squinted at the youngest member.

"Mr. Christopher and Susan?" asked Anna.

Hunter nodded, glancing back at Mrs. Emily and Birmingham. "Mr. Christopher called the man Mr. Crutcher and told him not to touch his clock or bother our house ever again or he would haunt them."

Brice looked from his son to Mrs. Emily and Birmingham, now making their way down the walkway.

"Couldn't of said it any better, Mr. Brice," replied Birmingham. "I saw both of 'em. The girl, Judy, ran off with the car when Mr. Clarence lit his pipe in front of the one called James."

"Yep," added Mrs. Emily. "And he done took off with little Susan holdin' the door open for 'em." Last we saw of James, he was runnin' down the road toward Munford."

"Come on in," said Birmingham. "But be forewarned, this place got more life in it than a mosquito pond." He looked to Anna. "We gonna need that little piece o' paper the Green Lady left upstairs. It got somethin' to do with that old clock."

"I'll get it," said Anna as she and Hailey trotted past the others and on toward the front porch.

"I'm going to call the Munford Police," grumbled Brice, now walking toward the house himself. "Our contact with the Crutcher family stops right now," he added as Heather and the others followed him into the living room.

Hearing the girls as they returned back down the stairs, Birmingham squinted as they slowed dramatically upon entering the dining area.

"All right, what's up now?" he asked, noting the puzzled look upon their faces as they stopped at the living room entrance.

"I smell the Grandfather's pipe," said Anna as Hailey nodded the silent echo.

Birmingham slowly turned toward the old timepiece. "Yep. I think I smell it too."

Mrs. Emily nodded with, "You don't think. . ."

Mrs. Emily's voice trailed off as her gaze made its way to Hershey. He was sitting at Hunter's feet who had just sat down on the couch next to the windows. The Labrador was staring at the clock also.

"Hershey can't tell time, Mr. B," said Hunter. "Somebody's still with us."

Just as hunter said that, the Labrador's gaze slowly made its way from the clock, past the china cabinet, and then to the couch behind him.

57

"Or her," corrected someone now sitting so close to Hunter it made him jump.

"Susan!" Hunter immediately scooted over a little, creating a comfort zone between him and the little ghost. "I didn't think you would still be here."

Birmingham stepped close to the back of the couch on the other side of the coffee table. Eying Susan, he patted the couch as if it were alive. "Is Mr. Clarence here?" he finally managed.

Susan nodded, smiling slightly. "He brought me. But he said I couldn't help or say anything, only watch for now."

Brice squinted, eying the little ghost in the yellow, buttercup dress. "Help us with what, Susan?"

"That." She nodded toward the note in Anna's hand.

"Can you come and go anytime you like?" asked Hailey.

Susan slowly shook her head. "I'm helping Grandfather now. He has one more chore to do before we go back and I'm doing that for him right now."

Hailey and Anna joined the others near where Birmingham and Mrs. Emily was standing.

"We've got it," said Anna as she handed the note to her father.

Brice took the note, noting the Smile on Susan's face. "You had something to do with us finding this didn't you?"

"Did I?" Susan's smile held.

"I got this." Hailey took paper. "She's playing hard to get."

"I think. . ." Heather paused, looking over Hailey's shoulder at the note. "The Grandfather is playing games with us."

"Well, read it," suggested Anna.

Hailey nodded and then read:
"As sure as one stands before the hands
And stares at the Oenothera,
You'll be but a reach from the aureus to keep
If you navigate its petals with kara. . . .
Start at noon, then pistol two petal."

"I hate riddles," grumbled Hunter, slouching back into the couch.

"Ohhh no," let's look at this," said Heather. "Mr. Clarence was very smart I think. He gave us kind of a map, but protected it with words. For instance; what does 'stands before the hands' mean?"

"The hands of the clock," Anna walked over to the old timepiece, stopping but a reach from its face. "Like this." She looked back at Hailey.

"All right." Hailey looked back to the note. "What does oenothera mean?"

"I got that one." Birmingham walked briskly to the bookcase where the Collier's Encyclopedias were. "O, right?"

Hailey nodded.

Thumbing through the 'O' book, he stopped and looked up grinning. "It's Latin. It's a primrose."

"There it is." Anna pointed to the pink flower carved on a panel below the clock's face. "All right. It says that you'll be but a reach from the aureus to keep."

"Got that too." Mrs. Emily pulled out the Collier's book marked 'A'. "Right here," she said quickly. "It means gold – a coin or ingot."

"Great Scott?" exclaimed Brice, now looking at the paper in Hailey's hands also. "It then says to navigate the petals with kara."

"Here we go again." Birmingham grabbed the 'K' book. A smile quickly formed on his face. "Old Mr. C likes to play games. That's Saxon for care."

"Now, we're at the last part and it doesn't rhyme," noted Hailey. "Start at Noon, then pistol to petal.'

"He's talkin' 'bout the flower," explained Mrs. Emily.

"Really?" Anna squinted at the six inch by ten inch carving on the clock. "It's the only thing carved on the clock."

Brice left Hailey's side and joined Anna at the clock. "The edged of the flower is carved very deep," he noted. "It's like he was trying to separate each petal from the clock and the center.

Anna looked back at Susah. Her grin was much wider than before. "Perhaps he did," she said, looking back at the clock. "We start at noon?"

"Yes," agreed Brice, but I don't think he talking about the clock's face right now."

Anna smiled, noting Susan's was also. "It's the primrose."

Anna slowly reached forward and pressed the petal at the top of the flower. When she did, the petal sunk in, releasing something inside the clock with a loud snap causing Anna to quickly jerk her hand back.

"My-my," said Birmingham, easing closer to the two at the clock. "So it all comes down to this? The Green Lady was after whatever's in the clock?"

Hailey nodded, with "Now pistol to petal."

"The center," said Anna excitedly. "Pistols are in the middle of the flower." She reached forward and pushed the center part of the carving.

The center gave, releasing the same, snapping sound inside the old clock.

"I got it! I got it!" exclaimed Hailey. "The next to the last word in that line is written as a number and not a preposition. It's t-w-o and not t-o. Push the second petal, Anna," she said excitedly.

"Wait a minute!" said Birmingham just as Anna reached toward the rose. He pulled out the Double Eagle from his pocket and kissed it. Looking at Brice, he added, "Don't know how much it's rightly worth, Mr. Brice. Some say from ten thousand dollars to a quarter of a million. Jus' depends on how new it looks." He nodded at Anna. "We're ready. Push it."

And so Anna did, creating the same snapping sound. But this time, the top of the panel containing the primrose carving opened slightly.

Hunter eased from the couch to join Birmingham and the others at the clock as Anna eased the panel door down and open.

"What are they?" asked Anna, staring at two, copper cylinder-shaped containers about the size of a half-dollar. Resting in carved out places in the wood, they were held down by a dowel wedged across their top from holes in each side of the clock.

"I got this," said Brice. He reached in, and forced the dowel backwards, releasing the cylinders. Picking one up, he looked back at the others with, "They're really heavy," he said as he unscrewed the top.

"What's in it?" asked Heather, noting his father had frozen with his mouth slightly agape.

Brice turned to face the others and let the gold coins slide out in the palm of his left hand.

"Ohhh my God," said Heather weakly as she leaned against Birmingham. But now remembering who was sitting beside her son, she wheeled back toward the couch at the windows. Susan, still smiling, was starting to fade--now, almost transparent.

"Do you have to go?" asked Hunter, noticing her condition also.

She slowly nodded, but kept the smile. "What you have just found was what Grandfather called his last chore. They're in the right hands now. Don't worry about the Crutchers. The police have them both and are now looking for their mother."

With those words, she gave a reluctant wave and then disappeared without a sound.

At that very instant, the old, grandfather clock struck twelve noon, causing Birmingham to jump. Facing it, he stood stone still until it struck twelve times.

"It's 1:00AM," noted Anna. "The Grandfather's clock is wrong?"

Handing the second cylinder to Brice, Birmingham closed the secret panel and then opened the face door of the clock. As he carefully adjusted its hands, he added, "Guess Mr. C's gone for good now." He looked back to Brice. "If it's all the same to all here, I'd like to take care of it from now on."

He slowly turned to get their response. All were nodding, even Hunter. But what caught his eye then, was the big, Chocolate Labrador had moved right up next to Hunter. The soft glow in his eyes was back.

"Uhhh. . .Mr. Brice?" Birmingham's voice weak. "Did she say for now?"

The End

www.ingramcontent.com/pod-product-compliance
Lightning Source LLC
LaVergne TN
LVHW012037060526
838201LV00061B/4646